Secrets Under the Stairs

by Karen Nolley

IEM TEXAS
Island Entertainment Media

Dedication

*I dedicate this book to
my family near and far,
with love.*

For comments or appearances from the author, please contact IslandEntertainmentMedia@gmail.com . Or visit www.IslandEntertainmentMedia.com.

Produced, Distributed, & Published by:

IEM Texas

1001 N. Travis
Sherman, TX 75090
©2015 Produced, Distributed, & Published by Island Entertainment Media
ISBN-13: 978-0692555422 (Island Entertainment Media)
ISBN-10: 0692555420

Visit Island Entertainment Media on the World Wide Web at
www.iemTexas.com

Secrets Under The Stairs

Chapter 1

My day started early this morning like every other work day - in much need of a morning shower to help me wake up. After showering and then walking around in my bath towel, I have my first cup of coffee. I do my hair, fix my makeup, brush my teeth, get dressed, and now I am finally heading out the door to work. I am a bookkeeper for a small CPA firm which is about thirty miles from Old Mills Hollow. That's where I live, so the drive seems forever when I get stuck in traffic. There are many industrial businesses along the road I travel to and from work. Along with the businesses comes the big trucks entering and exiting the road, which causes a lot traffic delays. At work, there are only two people that work in the office besides me. Making copies, organizing, and reviewing finances are just some of many that my job entails. My schedule is like clockwork. Since my schedule is pretty much the same each day, it feels like they run together. The radio came on when I started my car. Today's weather forecast calls for cloudy skies with severe thunderstorms. I'm not fond of storms at all, and I do not like driving in them either. Driving to work, on the left side and a few yards from the road, there is a two story house with a fenced in yard. This house catches my eye every day that I drive by it. It is a Victorian style house with colors of dull green and burgundy. It would be a beautiful house if it was better taken care of. As I get closer, the house has this creepy and mysterious look to it. With grey clouds twisting and turning as they hover in the sky above the house, it gives off an aura - as if the house were haunted. I wonder what history this house has. I want to know more. For as long as I have worked out of town, I have never really noticed much change while driving by. I am not really sure why it catches my eye, or why I am really even curious about the house. Not too many things catch my interest of that kind. Within the last four weeks I have observed a few different things about the house when passing by. The tall weeds that are growing taller on the outside of a white picket fence that surrounds the house for example. The fence is in need of repair and repainting. Also, a crooked tree that stands on the east side of the house and inside the fence. It has a rope hanging from one of the branches. Vehicles are never there. At least from what I can tell from the road. It is the most peculiar of houses that I have ever seen.

It's now after lunch, and I am all caught up with paperwork. I will just sit here and listen to the radio while I wait to see if my boss needs anything else. I may go home early. While listening to the Weather Channel on the radio at work, they stated that Old Mills Hollow and surrounding counties were under a severe thunderstorm warning for a fifty mile stretch. I leaned over to the window in my office. The sky is dark with grey clouds. The wind is blowing trees over and the thunder is loud and constant. I think I will leave a few minutes early to head home before the weather is too bad to drive in. I straighten my desk and go to tell my boss that I am leaving early. Before I can get a word out, Diane shouts from her desk, "You may go ahead and leave Lexi. It looks nasty out there and I don't want you to get caught up in the storm."

"Yes ma'am, I will see you tomorrow," I responded.

As I step out onto the sidewalk under the awning, the rain lets up a bit, but is falling at a slant due to the wind. I use my umbrella and run to the car, splashing in the puddles as I get closer. Fondling for my keys in my purse, I finally find them and get in the car. My car starts up with no problem and now I am headed home. The wind is blowing so hard I have to drive extra slow just to stay on the road. I am so close to Old Mills Hollow. Suddenly, there is a lot of traffic slowing down but there is none coming from the other direction. As I am going with the flow of traffic, which is very slow, an ambulance and two police cars pass me by. There must be an accident up ahead because now traffic is at a halt. A few minutes have gone by and I am still sitting at a standstill. I turn my car off and turn the radio up. None of the stations are coming in and the rain is getting heavier, and the raindrops are larger than I have seen before. I look around, and it just so happens that I am stopped right in front of the creepy old house. As I am sitting here, I just stare at the house. I notice many windows, and that the house is in dire need of a paint job and cosmetic work. When looking at the upstairs window, I see the shadow of a person who looks like they have fallen.

I pull my car over out of traffic in front of the house. I try to call 911, but I can't get through because of the weak cellular signal. Deep in the pit of my stomach I am feeling nervous, anxious, and somewhat scared. The rain is falling harder, and I'm sitting here thinking, "Should I go get help and what would I tell them?" I may have seen someone fall in their home, but I don't know who they are or anything about the person"

I thought to myself. I'm not sure that I would believe that story if someone came up to me. I go on to ask myself, "should I go see if they need help?"

While I sat for a minute, it began to hail and sounded as if the windshield was going to crack. It hails for about five minutes, then slows down and stops. When the rain lets up some, and with every impulse of my being, I get out of my car and run towards the house using my jacket to shield me from the rain. I cannot get through the gate, so I walk to the side of the fence where it wasn't so tall and climb over.

As I walk up the stairs to the front door, I have to be careful not to step on the broken boards of the porch. It is badly in need of repair. I am dripping wet from running in the rain. I knock on the door twice and then wait a few seconds. No one answers. I knock again. Still no answer, but I can hear something. I can hear a faint noise, but I can't tell what it is exactly. The porch wrapped around so I go to the right side of the house and I notice a window is open. I lean in through the window a bit and yell, "Is there anyone there? Are you ok?"

Again, no answer. I took my shoes off and put them through the window and climb through. I get through, and as I am putting my shoes back on I scream out, "Hello? Anyone here? My name is Lexi, Lexi Alan, and I am here to help you. I was passing by and thought I saw someone fall."

No one answered. I took a minute to walk around the room. It is an office or a study. Everything in this room is in neat order, but has dust on it and does not look like it has been touched in years. There is an antique desk with various items on it; a bust glass paperweight of someone, pen and pencil set, and a tray with folded newspapers in it. On the front page of the paper is the date April 16, 1969 in red.

The study is very organized with shelves full of books, old maps, and pictures on the walls. There is an old picture of a man above the fireplace. It is a black and white picture, and he looks very distinguished. He is wearing a suit holding a pocket watch in one hand, and the other pointing a finger as if he is pointing in a specific direction. It is a side profile of his face with no smile, just a serious stare portraying that he may be angry.

Also in the study, there is a small seating area near the corner of the room. I walk over to the high back chair and look over to notice a very unique table. The table that sits in front of and between two chairs, is a glass top table with an antique collection of toy guns under the glass. The table is a neat way to display such items. They would make for a good subject to an opening conversation. I turn around and proceeded through the doorway into the hallway.

Across from me, I see what looks like could be a living room. I walk to the French doors to look through, but could not quite see because of the curtains. I knock on the glass but no one answers. I jiggle the door handle and the door will not open. The door is locked. To my left is the front door and to my right is a stairway that leads up to the second floor. Beside the stairwell is a long narrow hallway, but I can't see where it leads. I walk upstairs since it looked like the person was on the second floor when they fell.

"Hello? Anyone there?" I shouted while going up the stairs. As I am walking, I notice many pictures. Some are of landscapes, one has an old well, and many group photos that look like family photos. There is a group photo in black and white of the man I saw in the photo downstairs above the fireplace. With him is a woman and two young boys.

When I get to the top of the stairs, I look to my right - there is a light shining out from under a door. I walk up to the door and knock but no answer. I open the door and it is a room decorated for a little boy. It is thoroughly clean, and there was not a speck of dust anywhere. That is strange to me since the first room I was in looked like it had not been cleaned in years. Someone made sure this room was well kept. "I wonder why someone would choose one room of a house to keep clean and not clean the entire house," I said to myself. The room had an old nautical theme to it. There are two twin beds that are fixed, and they have sailboats on the blankets, as well as on the curtains that are hanging up in the windows. There is an antique toy train set displayed on a table. It has elaborate details with a little town that has people and everything. I walk over to the closet and open the door. There are shoes organized on the floor and small clothes hanging up. If I had to guess, I would say this room is for a little boy around four or five years old. There is an old wagon with small animals in it, and two slingshots hanging on the wall. I wonder where the boys are.

I walk out of the room and down the hallway to the next door, which is open. I step in, turn on the light and scream so loud I almost go hoarse. There is a tall, swivel mirror in front of me. When I turned on the light, I thought that someone was there, but it was only my reflection. Boy do I feel stupid. I open the door all the way and see that everything is covered with white sheets. In the far corner on the left side of the room is something oddly shaped and covered. I go over to it and lift the sheet. It was an old baby cradle with a few stuffed animals, a folded baby blanket, and an old picture frame with two pictures in it. One is of a baby, and the other is of a little boy. He looks like the boy in one of the pictures on the wall of the stairwell. I covered the cradle back and look around the room some more. There aren't any pictures on the walls, just a large room with furniture that had sheets on them.

There is another door on the other side of the room, so I walk over to open it. This room is a bathroom decorated neatly in Victorian style with lace curtains and beautiful floral lace wallpaper. On the counter is a woman's hairbrush, mirror, and comb set - all in gold setting. The bathroom is large with the commode in its own small room in the corner. I thought to myself, "Whomever built this house was thinking of privacy." The bathtub was built into the floor. One would have to step down to get in. I have never seen this before. There are old melted down candles on the floor, along with a champagne bucket and a drinking glass by the tub that is laying sideways on the floor. When I get closer to the bathtub, I notice dark green broken glass, and a large oddly shaped brown rust stain in the tub. There is also a large splatter of rust on the floor outside of the bathtub and goes up along the wall. Everything looks like it has been here for a while, and is very dusty like the study.

I am starting to feel uncomfortable inside and I almost forgot the main reason why I am in this house in the first place. Immediately walking out of the bathroom and out of the bedroom, I walk to the end of the hall to the last door. I grab the doorknob to open it, but it is locked.

All of the sudden, the lights go out. I start to panic. It is so dark I can't see my hand in front of my face. I put my hands on the wall and follow the wall back to the stairs. I slowly walk down the stairs - still keeping my hands on the wall and trying to keep from falling. When I get to the bottom of the stairs, I turn around to my right and take two steps. Suddenly, I feel something touch my back and then a quick sharp pain to the back of my head.

Chapter 2

My eyes begin to open slowly. Everything is a blur, but I can make out some things. I am lying on the floor of a dark room and my head is throbbing. I sit up little by little, and put my hand on the back of my head. I then move my hand in front of my face, and there is a wet substance on my hand but I can't see what it is. I just know its blood. Someone hit me hard with some kind of a rigid object. I get up and put my hands out to feel around. I am extremely wobbly and unsteady. I take a couple of steps and I can feel the door to the dark room. With my hands on the door, I move one hand around to find the knob. I jiggle the doorknob, but it is locked. Terrified to death, I begin to panic.

I start yelling and beating on the door. "Please let me out of here. Please, I mean you no harm!"

I didn't hear a sound. I continue beating on the door until I got tired, then sat down and cried. I am so frightened. Many thoughts start running through my head. Are they going to kill me? I don't know what they want with me. I can only imagine what he - or they, will do to me. How many are there? I lean up against the door, banging and crying more and more, and still nothing.

"I wish I would have never stepped foot in this house," I cried out.

It felt like several minutes had gone by. I need to pull myself together so I can find a way out of here. My head is pounding from being struck by an object and from crying. Even though I have a bad headache, I stop crying and begin looking around. I need to find something that I can use to pry the door open with, or use to pick the lock. There is a little bit of light coming from underneath the door, so I start looking around the area of the door to see what I can find. I use my hands, moving them around on the floor while crawling on my knees.

While looking, I knock a box over and make a huge mess. I push most of what fell out of the box over to the light from underneath the door. Maybe I can find something of good use. Rummaging around, I found a small lighter. I strike the lighter a few times and it finally lights. I move everything away from the door and scoop it all back in the box using the lighter to see. Then I walk around trying to find a light, or light switch to turn on. It is hard to use the lighter to see for too long because it gets so hot, it burns my finger. While walking around to find a light switch, a string hits me in the head. I use the lighter to see.

When I look up, I notice it is a string to a light. Finally, I found a light and pull the string down.

The small light lights up the room. It isn't very bright, but enough so that I can see around me. The room is a small, long and narrow closet that is very dirty and is cluttered with boxes, frames, and old furniture. There aren't any windows, and really isn't much room to move around in here. I begin shoving things around and looking through boxes to see what I can use to open the door with. As I am digging through stuff, I find quilts, lots of old pictures of many sizes, boxes within boxes, and a strange looking key. Nothing big or strong enough to get through the room door. I grab the key and I go over to the door to see if the key can unlock the door, but it would not fit. I put the key in my pocket in case I can use it later.

I start looking through the old photographs and find some photos of two little boys. In many photos, the boys are wearing matching outfits and shoes. The same boy in each photo is not smiling while the other boy is.

"I guess the boy not smiling does not like having his picture taken," I thought to myself. These boys must be the boys that have the room upstairs that I walked into when I first arrived. I stop looking at the photographs and continue to look around. In the back corner of the room, I find a square door in the wall. I place both of my hands on the door and pull to open it, but it's locked. I use the lighter to give more light. As I move the lighter around, I find a key hole. Remembering I had found an unusual key earlier, I dig it out of my pocket. I put the key in the key hole and turn it. I put my hands on the door and pull it. It opens!

I lean in, putting my head through the opening. It's an old dumbwaiter. Maybe I can use this to escape from this closet. Suddenly, I hear a noise. It is the sound of what I think is the front door opening then closing shut. He is back! I close the door to the dumbwaiter quietly and go back towards the closet door. I am standing up against the wall away from the door. The door opens to the closet and a man hands me a bottle of water and a small paper bag.

"Put the trash by the door when you are done," he said. Then he stated, "If you need to use the bathroom, there is a small room you can access through the wall."

He points to the wall behind me. "You can figure it out." He then slams the door to the closet and locks it back. I open the bag and there is a burger and a bag of chips. Food. I am confounded. Trying to get out of this place is all I need to worry about, so I sit on the floor thinking about how I am going to get out of here.

Secrets Under The Stairs

While sitting on the floor a few minutes, my stomach begins to make noises. I move some boxes and an old shelf over. I take the shelf and lay it over on top of the boxes face down to make a small table. There is a small crate, so I grab it to use as a stool. I lean up against the wall and begin to eat. Then suddenly, the wall I was leaning on seems loose and moves a little. I moved some boxes away from the wall and place my hands on the wall to push. I lean towards the wall and push as hard as I can but it will not hardly budge. I put my back up against the wall and push with all my might. I am able to move the wall enough to get through the opening.

There is so much dust and cobwebs. The wall is actually an old door to another room. The place where the door knob used to be was removed and the hole was filled in. This is what the man was talking about earlier when he mentioned the bathroom. I walk in through the opening to the other side of the wall and notice a stairway. I strike the lighter to get more light and walk along the wall down the stairway, hoping to find a light switch. It is very dark going down, and a little colder than the other room. I stir up so much dust coming through the wall that I cough uncontrollably for a minute. I get to the bottom of the stairs, and go to the right along the wall. I bump into some boxes that are stacked along the side of the wall. I continue to follow the wall in front of the boxes. At the end of the line of boxes I find a switch.

When I turn the switch on, I am in complete disbelief. It is a small room with cement walls. There is an old metal, twin size bed at one corner with a table and lamp beside it. In the other corner is a small sink with a mirror hung on the wall above it, and a commode beside the sink. On the edge of the sink is a small bottle of soap. I look around some more and I can see something on the wall beside the bed. I go over by the bed to see what it is and I can't believe my eyes. It is a chain attached to the wall. Someone was being held here and was bound by chains. I became overwhelmed with terror and quickly run back upstairs. I close the door to the room, and put everything back against the wall so that it doesn't look like I found the room. My heart is racing and I can barely catch my breath. Food has been the farthest thing on my mind, but I am starving. I sit back at the table to finish eating. Sometime later, I am feeling extremely tired, light headed, and nauseated. I drop what little was left of my burger and fall over the table.

The next day I wake up and I am feeling lethargic and just heavy - like something is weighing me down. Then I notice my clothes. They are not mine. He must have put something in my food that made me pass out and then changed my clothes. I am wearing a white gown and my hair has been brushed and is pulled back in a clip. I run over to the door and start beating on the door yelling, "Why are you doing this to me?" But there is no answer. "Oh no," I thought. The key I found was in my pocket. If he checks my pockets, he may figure out what I want to do, or am thinking of doing. Then I immediately become relieved because I remember that I had left the door to the dumbwaiter unlocked.

I can't believe he changed my clothes. I wonder, "Why did he pick out this type of clothing to put on me?" I need to get back to figuring out how to get out of here, but first I have to use the bathroom. I move everything away from the wall and open the door. I go back down the stairs. This is so creepy. I hope there isn't any cameras down here. As I sit down to use the bathroom, I look around the room. I look in the upper corners of the ceiling, and anywhere else that could possibly have a camera. That is the fastest I have ever used the bathroom before. I hustle to wash my hands, then hurry back upstairs leaving the door open.

I know I have only been here a day, but I need to find a way to keep track of how long I am here. I start keeping a calendar in the far corner of the closet. After each meal, I will make a mark and maybe that will help me keep up with how many days I am here. Hopefully that won't be very long. So far I have had one meal that includes a burger which made me pass out. I don't know if I should eat anything else he gives me. Drugging my food was sneaky. And to do that in order to change my clothes. Although, it is strange that this man kidnaps me and is taking care of me. I haven't heard of many captors that take care of their prisoners while being held. "Is he keeping me alive for something," I whisper to myself. Listening to my gut is what got me in this mess, and I need to figure a way out of it. He left me in here, but for what? Has he taken me hostage for entering his house unlawfully or does he have an alternative motive? I wish I would not have come.

Still feeling dazed and out of sorts, I go back over to the dumbwaiter to see if I can use it to get out of this room. I stack some sturdy boxes up against the wall below the door to the dumbwaiter. I open the door then stand on the boxes. I look in and I can see up and down the shaft. I know I have two directions in which to go. The shaft is dusty, cold, and has cobwebs everywhere. Not sure, but it looks like it has not been used in a long time. Going up seems more logical in order to find the nearest exit so I will go up. I crawl in the shaft and position myself so that I can crawl up the shaft, hopefully quietly. It is a very tight space, but I can fit. My feet slip about every other inch or two that I move. This is not going to be easy. I reach for the first door I come to and open it. I can hear something. I brace myself in a way to hold myself up. There is a small hole so I lean into it to look. As I am propping myself in the shaft trying to stay up, I slip and lose one of my shoes, causing it to bounce off the sides of the walls. Suddenly, I hear footsteps then the door to the shaft opens. It's the man that put me in the closet. He puts his hands in and tries to grab me. As we struggle, I lose my grip and fall down the shaft a few feet. As I am falling, I brace the sides of the opening I crawled in to keep from falling further. I climb out of the shaft, close the door to it, and run over by the wall. I become aware of cuts on my arm and leg. I go over to the box and grab a small blanket. I tear it into strips, then wrap the strips around both of the cuts. I tie them off to help stop the bleeding. I head back over by the wall and sit up against it. Time seems to go by slowly, when all of the sudden, I hear footsteps walking towards the closet door. He opens the door, then pushes a tray of food and water towards me. Then he says, "If you try that again, you will regret it." Scared and crying I yell out to him, "Why are you doing this to me?"

He runs at me with his arm raised up high and swings down striking the right side of my cheek. He then says, "Shut your mouth, and don't try anything stupid."

He turns around and walks out- slamming the door shut and locking it. I'm sitting here with my hand over my cheek - holding it and crying. The sting from being slapped is slowly going away.

After a few minutes of crying, I get up and go to the downstairs area of the hidden room to look in the mirror. My cheek is red and a little warm. I wipe away the tears from my face and head back upstairs. The tray has a mixture of muffins and donuts. I grab the tray and water, then go over to the make-shift table I had made and sit on the old crate. I open the bottle of water and take a drink, and have a bite of the muffin. A few minutes go by before I realize I have eaten a couple of muffins and drank a whole bottle of water. After that, I go to sit on the floor so I can glance through some more boxes. I start to feel tired. I could barely keep my eyes open. I begin opening one of the boxes and before I know it, my body feels extremely heavy and I fall over on the box.

After some time has passed by, I open my eyes. I feel like I have been out for a while. I sit up and look around. He has laid me on a quilt and covered me up. I throw the blanket from my legs. I notice the strips I had put around my arm and leg when I cut myself were replaced with fresh bandages. He must have put something in my food again! I am feeling frustrated. Why can't he just tell me what he wants with me? I go over to the small table, and I can see that the tray has also been replaced. I remove the cover from the tray. There is bacon, eggs, and toast along with orange juice and more water. "Why is he bringing me more food?" I said confusingly but in a low tone. It hasn't been long since I ate last. I don't know if I should eat anything else he gives me. It seems when I eat, I fall asleep and wake up later finding out that something has changed, or has been done to me. It all smells so good, and I am a little hungry. Maybe if I space it out and not eat all of it at once, it won't affect me much if he has put something in the food.

I start to eat. I have a piece of bacon, two bites of eggs, and then a half piece of toast. Suddenly, I hear footsteps coming towards the closet door. I quickly grab a blanket and lay back down on the quilt. I turn over and cover my face a little and act like I am asleep. I can hear the sound of the door unlocking and the knob turning. My body is cringing with fright. I feel the footsteps on the floor coming towards me. Even though I am frightened, I lay still and do not move. The footsteps stop. I can hear the noise of him rummaging through something. Then the footsteps lead away from me. The door closes and I hear it lock.

I wait a minute then quietly sit up and look around. He took the tray and left. So much for eating a little here and there.

That was a close one. Then I said with a whisper, "I wonder who was being detained in the basement room? I have got to figure a way out of here. I do not want to be the next person he puts down there. I need to know what I am up against here, so think! What should I do?"

I start looking around, noticing all of the things in the closet. What there mostly is here, is boxes. So I pick a box and start examining it. I tear open the tape on the top of the box. I begin digging through the box and notice it is folders of outdated medical records. As I look closer, I can see they're records for the same person. A boy named of Daniel. In one of the folders I opened, Daniel was seen for a broken arm, and there was a description section where they had noted bruising on his chin. He was only one year old. Wow! I wonder what happened to cause him to break his arm. In comments, it states he fell from the top bunk. That is strange because if Daniel is the one who shares the boys' room in this house that I had seen, there is not a bunk bed in there. With my curiosity getting the best of me, I put the folder back in the box and grab another folder. The doctor's report states in this record that Daniel suffered a concussion, and fractured his wrist as a result from falling down the stairs. The report also states Daniel has bruising on his upper and lower back, as well as the upper thigh of his right leg. This boy is either very clumsy or there is foul play involved. I put the folder back in the box and close it back the way I found it. I put the box back in the stack with the other boxes, and grab another one. This one has a lot of old photographs. Some amount of time has gone by as I continue to look through the box. There are many family photos, and some photos of two little boys. I keep digging through the box and find an old book. It is faded on the outside with flowers on it, and a rubber band around it. I take the rubber band off and open the book. It is a diary or journal of some sort. I hear footsteps coming towards the closet door again. I immediately close the box, push it back with the others, and go sit on the crate by the table I made earlier. I tuck the journal behind me in between the wall and crate. The door screeches open and the man walks inside. He is carrying a stack of clothes with some sandals. He puts it down on the floor by the door and looks around. He says in an abrupt enraged tone, "No funny business. Don't think about trying anything stupid or you will regret it."

Then he leaves the room and locks the door behind him. The sound of his voice is terrifying. It's a deep voice that is difficult to describe, but not a voice you want to hear over your shoulders in the dark indefinitely. I am not sure how much longer I can take being here.

Secrets Under The Stairs

With all the marks I have on the wall, it seems I have been here almost three days now, but it feels like more. I have managed to reorganize the closet making it roomier, so that I can keep track of what I have gone through. Remembering that I hid the journal I found the other day, I walk over to the table and dig it out from the hole in the wall. I take the journal and sit at the table to read while I eat. I take the cover from the plate. It is soup of some kind, with a sandwich and crackers. I begin to eat. I take a quick look through the journal before reading the first entry, and I notice each entry is dated. The first entry is long, and goes on to talk about her sons needing to get along. From what I gather reading this, the mother was stressed from trying to be the peacemaker between the two boys, and the father was out of town a lot. One sentence stated: "How can one boy be so sweet and delightful to be around, and the other boy be so opposite and scary to be around."

A picture fell out of the back of the journal. It was a picture of one son with an inscription on the back:

"My dear sweet Daniel, I love and miss you so much."

So this is a picture of Daniel, and it is the same boy that the medical records were about. I said to myself, "I wonder if the emergency room and doctor visits I saw in the medical records really were accidents."

I began reading more of the journal. In another entry the mother describes how she is scared to go to sleep at night because she is afraid of what David might do. David must be the name of the other boy. She goes on to describe the relationship between her and the boys. She locks herself in the bathroom and writes, while soaking in the bathtub with a glass of wine. This could explain why there is broken glass by the tub. She may have been the one who dropped the glass or tipped it over and broke it while in the tub. I'm just guessing though. Who knows what really happened.

I finish eating and straighten the area where I ate. Then I put another mark on the wall behind the boxes to mark how long I have been here.

Another day goes by, so now it has been four days and I can't help but wonder if someone is looking for me. I need to find a way out of here. I go to the back of the closet to the dumbwaiter. I open the door to it and crawl in. I start climbing up. As I am ascending, I go past the first door that I had come to when I tried this before. Being as quiet as I can, I keep climbing up. I come to another door. I look through the little hole that you put your finger through to open the door, and I try to see if I can find anyone. There is no one, as far as I can tell. I can't hear anything either, so I slowly open the door. I move my right leg up first, then I put it through the doorway and climb out. There is a small wooden table below the doorway to the dumbwaiter that I use to step out on to. As I climb out, I knock over a vase of flowers and it breaks. Many pieces of glass scatter in different directions. I quickly look around to find something to keep me from cutting myself when I pick up the glass. I grab a large piece of cloth from a small table and use it to pick up the shards of glass then put it in a box nearby. I then close the box and make sure it was how I found it. I am hoping he would not know I was here.

I begin to look around. I am in the attic. As I stand here, I look around trying to notice everything I possibly can. There is a small window on the other side of the attic. I quietly walk over to the small window and look out. "I can see the front yard that faces the highway!" I say with excitement. The window isn't a logical place to escape. It is too high up. As I look more, I remember I left my car on the side of the road in front of the house. I look for my car but it is not where I left it. I wonder where it is - my car could have been towed; could he have moved it? It's been a few days, so it is possible he moved it right after I was taken hostage. I wonder if anyone has reported me missing. Surely my office has since I never miss work, and I have not shown up in the last few days. I turn around and walk away from the window. There are a lot of things up here. On one side of the attic is an area set up neatly but there is a lot of dust. There is an antique vanity table with a bench, a tall mirror, and a tall armoire. It's as if someone plays dress up. I walk over to the armoire. I open the armoire and there are countless dresses hanging along with hats, bonnets, and fedoras on a shelf. Near the bottom of the armoire are two drawers. I kneel down to open the first drawer and I am shaken. There lays a knife partially wrapped in a cloth with old dried blood on the blade. It looks like it had been there for a lengthy amount of time. I was not expecting that. I became so startled that, while I am kneeling to look in the drawer, I fall back, landing on the floor. I am curious, is the man that captured me capable of killing, or did someone else do it and he is covering for them? I quickly close the drawer. I have been up here for a while. I need to get back down to the closet before he notices I'm gone.

I get up and scamper towards the opening of the dumbwaiter which is near the attic door. Before I climb in from the table, I reach over and try the door knob and it opens. With overwhelming excitement I immediately shut it back quietly and climb in the opening of the dumbwaiter. It's very tight in here, but I need to hurry. I brace myself tight with each motion. I pass the first door as I continue down. I reach the next door and climb out.

I am back in the closet. I start wiping myself off to remove the dust and cobwebs from my clothes. I move over and sit at the table then take a long drink of water. Trying to be quiet and quick can be an overpowering adrenaline rush. As I sit here, I keep thinking about the unlocked door in the attic, and also the knife. I could have used that knife for protection. When it's time, I need to get back up there and see if that is my way out of here. I can't believe I found a bloody knife- and in the strangest place too.

Feeling exhausted, I drink a little more water, then go over to grab a blanket. I lay it out to make a small pallet and grab another for a pillow. With a make-shift bed made, I lay down. I am so drained. As I lie here, many random thoughts start running through my mind. I know there is someone looking for me. Is he going to hurt me? Will I ever get out of here? I just need to stay strong, and try not to worry so much. The more I thought about all of it, the more tired and scared it made me.

Some time had passed as I began to wake up. I sit up and look around. Nothing looks disturbed or changed. It all looks the way I left it before I fell asleep. I got up, folded the blankets, and put them back with the other stack of blankets. I can hear someone coming. I go over to the table and sit down. I hear a door shut. "Is he leaving or is he coming in?" I ask myself. I go over by the door of the closet to listen. He is leaving the house. What a relief. I thought he was coming back in here.

I wait a few minutes to make sure he is not coming back in the house. No sound of the front door opening, I head back to the dumbwaiter. I crawl back in and I climb back up to the attic. I get to the top and climb out onto the small table where I jump down. I go to the door and turn the knob. It opens. I open the door slowly so that it would not make a noise in case someone else is here. Then I walk out of the attic and close the door quietly. I begin walking down the flight of stairs cautiously until I come to the first flat at the second floor of the stairs. I slowly turn the knob opening the door a bit to see out. I look around and listen closely to see or hear anything. I can't hear or see anything, so I continue walking down past the rooms to the stairway. I reach the bottom and look around the corner both ways, and still... nothing. The front door is right in front of me. I pause for a few seconds, nervous of what is, or what might be on the other side of the front door. I frantically run to the small window beside the door and peek out. I can see the gate to the yard. I look around some more and don't see anyone, so I go for the door. I slowly open it and peek out. I step out and run to the end of the porch. The fresh air from outside was overpowering, and the sunlight is so bright I can hardly see. The scent of the flowers are amazing. I was in that room for so long, I forgot what the outside was like.

As I am standing at the stairs of the front porch, I notice a large barn off to the side. I wonder if he put my car in the barn. It looks big enough to hold a car. I run down the steps and through the gate. Then I dart for the barn, looking both ways and behind, making sure no one is around. I reach the barn door and notice there is a lock on the door. I grab the lock and give it a tug, but it doesn't budge. I walk around to the left side of the barn. There is a stack of old wooden pallets. I got on one side of them, lean up against the stack with my back, and push them a few inches until I am able to line them up underneath a small window. I climb up on the stack to look through the window. There is debris and dirt all over the window. I stand up tall and use the lower part of my gown to wipe the window. Then I kneel down to look through and I can see what could be my car, but there is no way to tell by looking because of the large blue tarp covering it. I put my hands on the window and push the lower part of the window in, and it opens. I put my left leg in, and then my right. I climb in. I land on a long, antique wooden table. I jump down and run over to the object covered by the tarp. I pull part of the tarp back, and much to my surprise, it is my car. I try to open the door but it is locked. When I go around and try the other doors, they are locked also.

There is no way I can escape on foot. I need my keys to get away. I make sure the tarp is placed on the car exactly how I found it. Then I went around where I had stepped and back track to the window. I cover my tracks with a broken piece of wood. Quickly, I leap back on to the wooden table and climb back through the window. I gaze around to see if anyone was nearby, but there is no one. I hurriedly place the pile of pallets back where they were, and use the piece of wood to cover up any signs of evidence that would show I was ever here. Looking out towards the house and all around, I run back towards to the house. I reach the porch, and I quietly walk up the steps to the door. I can see in the window and everything looks transparent. I then quietly open the front door and walk in, while looking around making sure the man isn't close by. I have a random thought, "I wonder if the keys to my car are in the den? I need to go look."

My heart is racing. I run over to the desk. I look on the top of the desk first, and I notice a paper in the tray with the date *April 16, 1969* in red. I remember that paper from when I first came into the house. I pick up the paper and begin to read.

Secrets Under The Stairs

It is a copy of a front page newspaper article. As I read, it says there is not enough evidence to solve the murder of a young mother of two. It further states she was cut deep by glass, then drowned in the bath tub while being held under water. I wonder if the mother was killed upstairs in the bath tub where I found the broken glass. If so, that is probably a blood stain in the bath tub and not rust stains.

I became terrified and put the paper back in the tray. I open the middle drawer to the desk and start to rummage through it. I find my keys and pick them up. Then suddenly, I can hear something. The sounds of footsteps on the porch, coming from the side of the house. I quickly close the drawer. I pull the chair out from the desk and duck down, hiding under the desk and pulling the chair back. The front door opens and then closes. I hear the sounds of plastic rubbing together, and footsteps leading away from the den. They are now making their way down the hall. I can't hear anything, so I push the chair out and crawl out from under the desk. While pushing the chair back in, I hear him coming back down the hall. I grab the bust paperweight from the desk to use as a weapon, and quickly run quietly over to the side of the doorway that leads to the den. I'm standing up against the wall. He is walking over to the French doors. I peek around the corner, and he is unlocking the doors.

He opens one of the doors and walks in. It looks like a living room from what I can see. The man sits down in the chair and turns on the television. It sounds like he is opening a bag of some kind. I lean back in the den, nervous and hoping I am not caught. I slowly sit on the floor up against the wall waiting for my chance to get up the stairs back to the attic.

Several minutes go by, and still no sign of him leaving the living room. I get up and peek out again. I can see his feet. He is laid back in a recliner. Leaving the paper weight on the floor, I tiptoe over to the doors of the living room. I lean to the right and I can see he is sleeping facing in the opposite direction than where I am standing. I immediately turn around and go for the stairs. I keep my eyes on him as I walk up the stairs until I lose sight of him. I run softly down the hall to the attic door. I can't get back to the closet fast enough before I start hearing sounds again. I then climb onto the table and back into the dumbwaiter bracing myself in the space. Once I'm in I pull the door closed.

I scramble down, being careful not to slip and fall. I reach the opening to the closet. I put one leg through to brace myself in the opening. As I crawl out, my keys fall from my pocket down the shaft. I began to cry out, "Dang it!" I get out of the dumbwaiter, and pull the door closed. Without warning, the man grabs me. He has his arm around my neck, then turns me around and smacks me across the face with the back of his hand. I fall to the floor and put my arms over my head to protect myself. He then stands over me, pulling me by my hair. He holds a cloth over my mouth while I kick and fight to get away.

Chapter 3

Waking up and feeling unsteady, I sit up while still on the floor realizing that I am bound with rope around my wrists. I feel wobbly and I'm trembling. He must have put something in the cloth so when I breathed it in I would pass out. I try to move my wrists and hands to see if I can get them free from the rope. The rope is too tight. I wish I would have grabbed that knife from the attic. All of the sudden, the man opens the door and he's carrying a tray. He sits it down on the table and walks toward me. He has a knife in his hand. I start to scream and try to move away from him. "No please no!" I scream out. He reaches for my feet and pulls me around to grab my hands. He then cuts the rope and my hands became free. I'm not sure if I should say thank you or try to hit him. This man is screwy.

He said in a scruffy angry tone, "You will not try that again. I have fixed it so that you can't get out through the dumbwaiter."

He walks away, slamming the door loudly. Crying is all I can do at this point. Trying to get out of here is hopeless now. I was so close. I sit for a while crying- with my hands around knees, and my head down. I cry until I don't have it in me to cry any longer. The gown I'm wearing is soaked from my tears, and my nose is runny. I need to blow my nose and wipe my face.

I go downstairs to the hidden room, then I walk over by the closet door and grab something fresh to change into. The gown I am wearing has gotten dirty from running to and from the barn, and from just being in the barn. Then I think, "I hope he doesn't realize I took my keys from the study."

I get a fresh set of clothes and go back down the stairs of the hidden room to clean off before I change. I put the clothes on the bed, then strip down to my underclothes. I turn the water on. I grab a washcloth and soap, then lather it under the faucet. I begin to wash up, cleaning all of the dirt off. I dry off, then change my clothes. It's difficult, but I lean into the sink and rinse my hair the best I can. I squeeze the water out. I don't have a towel big enough to wrap my hair in, so I wring out as much water as I can. I have to use my fingers to comb through my hair.

I clutch the dirty clothes under my arm and make my way back upstairs. I place them on the floor by the closet door. I find a small rubber band and use it to make a ponytail so I can keep my hair out of my face. I should have done this the other day. I head over to the boxes along the wall, and start burrowing through them. As I move the boxes over to start digging through them, I notice a light coming from underneath the wall. I haven't noticed it before. I move more of the boxes over. I begin to touch and push on the wall, moving my hands all around.

"Maybe there is a way out after all", I think. Excitement comes over me while trying to figure out what the light is coming from. Then, suddenly, I find a weak spot in the wall. I push and push as hard as I can until the wall moves. I quickly jump up and put my head to the opening so I can see. It is hard to see through the small opening, but there are wooden work benches, tools hanging from the walls, and shelves full of junk. I shove the wall more, and I'm able to get through. I walk into the room and walk around to see if there is a way out. I realize this is the basement. Someone must have built a wall to separate the two rooms. This is a strange house, and a sinister man who lives here. There is a small, elongated window near the ceiling on the other side of the room. I can't reach it unless I stand on something to see out. I walk around some more, and I see a square opening in the wall. I walk towards it and realize it is the opening to the dumbwaiter that comes down to the basement. I remember I had dropped my keys earlier, and I immediately hit my hands and knees to start looking for them. I see them under the shelf, but I can't reach them. I need to find something to use to reach out. I find a long yard stick, and stick it under the shelf sideways. This does the trick, and I am able to reach them. I pull the yard stick out slowly from under the shelf and grab the keys. I am overjoyed. I put the keys in my pocket. I head over to the deep freezer near the window and against the wall. I try to push it under the window sill so I can stand on it, but the heavy appliance would not budge. I try to open it to see what's in the freezer, but there is a lock on it. I walk over to the tools on the wall and search to find something I can use to cut, or bust, the lock off of the freezer. I find a crow bar. I grab it and go back to the freezer. I put one end of the crowbar in the open space of the lock, and hold it on the other end. After a few rounds of pulling and yanking as hard as I can, the lock breaks off. I put the crowbar on the shelf behind me and turn to open the freezer door. When I open it, I could not believe my eyes. There is a frozen body of a human. It looks like a man, and he looks like he has been in here for a long time. Even though he is wrapped in clear plastic, I still can't make out his face. There is so much freezer burn. He has ice all over him. Now I know why the freezer would not move.

It's too heavy with the body and whatever else is in there. I quickly shut the freezer and hang the lock back on it to make it look like it's locked. I grab the crowbar and hide it by putting it under the opening in the wall, then pulling it closed. I don't even worry about putting the boxes back. At this point, I don't know what to do next, but I need to get out of here quick before something bad happens to me- or I end up like that man in the freezer.

I take the keys from my pocket and walk over to the box that has a lot of folded quilts in it. I hide the keys down in the box between the quilts. I am filled with so many emotions right now. Feeling optimistic, I think I can get out through the basement, either through the door up the stairs or the window somehow. I'll try again when I know I have enough time to attempt it, hopefully without him catching me next time.

Secrets Under The Stairs

Chapter 4

After all this time here, I still do not know what the man's name is. He has never told me. Thinking about that, I toddle over and sit down at the table. I take notice of the sound outside the closet. The door opens just enough for a hand to reach in and grab the clothes I left earlier, and replace them with more. The door locks back. I walk over towards the door and look at the clothes. Nothing different. Still the same style of clothing he has been leaving me. I bet these clothes belonged to the lady that was killed in the bathtub. I didn't touch them. I just walk back to the table and sit down. The tray the man left earlier, when he came in and cut the rope from my hands, is still untouched. There's a sandwich wrapped in plastic, along with chips, a cookie, and more water. I pull apart the sandwich and it is tuna fish. I look curiously at the sandwich. I notice there is discoloration in the tuna. I bet he mixed a drug in it. I take the sandwich, but leave the wrapper, and go to hide it. I find a stack of newspapers and wrap the sandwich in them. I then put it inside one of the boxes. I take two other boxes and stack them on top of this one- just in case. I never know what this man is thinking or going to do next. I can only speculate. I sit down at the table and start eating the chips, since they are in the original package, then drink some water. After eating, I just sit at the table. My mind keeps wandering, and it is making me tired. I have no momentum. It's hard to keep your energy up when you are confined in a small space without much to do. I unfold the quilt and lay it out. I use another one as a pillow and lay down. I fall fast asleep.

A few hours later, I wake up slowly and look around to find that the tray my sandwich had been on is still here, and nothing looks touched. I guess he is not eager to come in here and check on me. The only thing I think seems likely to work, is to go back into the basement if I want to get out of here. Somehow, I need to get to the small window and climb through so I get to my car. Then I can get the heck out of here. Timing is everything if I want to escape without getting caught again. I believe I will try it tomorrow when I know he is leaving the house. Hopefully he leaves the house tomorrow, or I will be here longer.

I can hear him doing something. I hear sounds with paper, as if he is rummaging through it or gathering it up. I am sitting at the table staring at the door of the closet. I can see a break in the light under the door. He's standing at the door.

The doorknob turns and the door opens. He walks in carrying a trash bag and heading towards the table. He has an outlandish look on his face as he gathers the trash I left from eating earlier. He doesn't say a single word. He just grabs the trash and walks out. I bet he was expecting me to be passed out from eating the sandwich.

As I am sitting at the table, I reach over into the small hole in the wall and grab the journal that I had hid, and begin to read it. I start where I left off from- the part where the lady has written about being scared of one of her sons, and would lock herself in the bathroom while taking a bath. The more I read, the more I find out she is terrified of being alone with this son. She goes on to write about how he picks on his twin brother often. It's obvious from all the things I have read, seen, and put together in my head - David and Daniel are bothers, and they are the boys who live, or have lived, in this house. One of them is the sweet, well-mannered one, and the other is the evil, trouble maker. I continue to read, turning page after page. David would hit birds with his slingshot, injuring them, then hanging them by their feet. He would then shoot them over and over until they were dead.

"That is awful," I think to myself. Towards the end of the book, I find an envelope taped to one of the pages. I open the envelope and pull out a letter.

I begin to read:

Secrets Under The Stairs

I am writing this letter to let someone know that my husband did not accidentally drown by falling in the bathtub. He was pushed by David, and all of the past accidents and trips to the doctor's office and emergency room visits that Daniel had were because of him also. He is evil and needs to be stopped. If you are reading this letter, it is because I am no longer here, and I can't go to my grave without letting someone know the truth about the death of my husband. I purposely made it appear that I could not take care of Daniel so that he would be put in foster care. At least I was able to save one person in my life. The death falls on my other son David. He is not well.

It goes on to state more, but I can't read anymore. This is shameful and terrifying. I wonder if he is going to kill me. "Please let me get out of here," I say in a low tone. I put the journal back by the table into the hole in the wall. I take the letter and fold it as small as I can, and put it underneath the strap of my bra. I tuck it into the front, below my shoulder. I definitely don't want David, if that is who is holding me here, to get ahold of this note. When I get out of here, I will get this in the right hands so that he does not get away with all that he has done. I need to stick to my plans of escape for tomorrow, and be sure not to give him any indication of my plans or what is going to happen.

Time has gone by and it's getting late. I am guessing that he will be coming in here soon. I need to keep calm and try not to act nervous so he will not be suspicious of anything. I go back over by the boxes and sit on the floor. I choose the box with an animal drawn on the side of it. After removing the lid from the box, I begin digging through it. I find some stuffed animals, old children's books, and many color pictures. I grab the pictures and commence looking through them. Most of the pictures are signed by Daniel. One in particular is a drawing of Daniel with his father and mother outside playing baseball together. David is not in this picture or any of the others. It's just the three of them. It's as if David didn't exist. I wonder if he was the one being held in the basement room because of his behavior, and the fact that his family feared him. It makes sense, but is pure speculation.

The man who may be David is at the door. I can hear him unlocking it. Before I can get everything back into the box, he walks in and explodes. He darts over to the table and places a bag on top. He then runs over to me, grabbing all of the things I had taken out of the box and shoving them back in. He closes the box and puts it back with the others. He screams in a deep voice with his hands raised at me as if he is going to strike me,

"Do not touch anything else!" Then he yells, "Stay out of things that don't belong to you, and nothing harmful will come of you!"

I sit still with my arms over my head for protection while he is yelling. He did not hit me. He just yells at me, then walks out slamming the door behind him. I slowly move towards the table hoping he is not coming back. I made him really angry. There are many different items and boxes in this room. I have a feeling he doesn't want me looking through anything because I may find something that I am not supposed to see. I am piecing some things together that, at this point, could only be considered speculation or circumstantial. Some things that I have read could be evidence of crimes committed if, in fact, this man really is David.

With all thinking aside, I open the bag to see what he left. He brought a barbeque sandwich with beans and a soda. It smells good, and it's still warm. I take everything out of the bag and place it on the table. I open each of the items, inspecting them and making sure nothing is tampered with. It all looks good, so I begin to eat. Not knowing what to really look out for, I only take a couple of bites of both the sandwich and beans. As I finish eating, I put all of my trash in the paper bag and put it over by the door of the closet.

I am sitting by the table thinking about tomorrow, and hoping my plans don't get interrupted. I can't spend another day or night in this place, and I need to make sure this letter I have gets into the right hands. There are just too many questions raised by the evidence and information that I have come across about what happened to the family in this house. For instance, the body down in the basement freezer that looks like it has been there for a long time. And then there's the letter I found in the back of the journal. Not to mention Daniel's medical records. I can't believe all that has happened in the past few days. Sitting here thinking about this is exhausting me. I go over to the boxes and grab the two quilts that I have been using to make a pallet. I lay the first one out, then the other on top, folding the upper part a few inches down. I get under the covers, and use my arm as a pillow to lay on. Again, I fall fast asleep.

Secrets Under The Stairs

Chapter 5

The next morning I woke up startled from a loud noise coming from outside. Hopefully he leaves the house, and soon. I don't know if I can stand to be here in this house another day. I fold the quilts and put them back in the box. I quickly notice a pile of folded and out dated clothing over by the door of the closet, along with another paper bag. He must have slipped the items in here while I was sleeping. When I begin looking through the clothing, I see he left a blouse with a skirt. He has only left me one pair of shoes- sandals. Either he doesn't know my size, or he doesn't want me to have them in case I try to escape. It's very strange because all of the items are my size.

"These clothes could be his mother's", I think. The clothes are similar styles to what I found in the armoire in the attic.

"Maybe she is similar in size to me."

I change my clothes and put the gown by the door. I grab the bag and take it to the table. He brought me a sausage biscuit, a bottle of juice, and a small bowl of fruit. I can still hear the loud noise coming from outside while I am eating. I can even feel a little vibration on the floor. It sounds like some type of construction equipment with beeping noises. I can only imagine what he is doing outside with that kind of equipment. I am exhausted, but on edge. My hope is slowly diminishing.

As I clean up my mess from eating, I change my thoughts to positive ones, and continue to speak out about my plan.

"I have to do this. No way am I going to stay even one more day in this place," I tell myself. I sit down after cleaning up, and I'm feeling more edgy and anxious. I take the letter that I hid under my bra strap, and begin to read it again. While I read the letter it helps me realize that I have to do this. Not only for myself, but so there is justice for what happened to this family. The man who is keeping me here needs to pay for what he has done to me, and for what he did to this family-if, in fact, he is the one that killed them. There is no doubt in my mind that he did it. If he is clever enough to kidnap and drug me, then there is no telling what else he is capable of doing. That tells me he thinks he has gotten away with his crimes, and I can't let that happen. I am going to sit here and wait until all is quiet and I know that he has left.

After a while, I stand up and stretch a minute. "Oh my!" I say with a worn out voice. "I must have dozed off for a few minutes."

I listen and can't hear a thing. The noise from the construction equipment has stopped. I wonder if he left. I went over to the door to see if I can hear anything.

"I can't hear a thing," I whisper under my breath. I stand here another minute or two, then I walk over to the dumbwaiter. As soon as I open the door to it, I hear the sound of the front door shutting. I quickly close the door to the dumbwaiter and run back over to the table. I sit down and listen some more. Then, unexpectedly, the door to the closet unlocks then opens. I am scared stiff. Beads of sweat begin to run down the sides of my face. My entire body begins to shake as the man walks in and says in a deep sounding voice, "Come here."

I slowly get up and walk toward him, trembling profusely. He hands me a bottle of water.

"Thank you," I respond after he hands it to me. He grabs the pile of clothes, and the bag of trash left from breakfast that I left by the door, then slams it shut. He doesn't say a word back to me. He just locks the door behind him.

I am still full from breakfast. It seems like I just finished eating.

I wonder, "is he leaving and that's why he gave me more food?".

Feeling restless, I head over to the closet door and sit on the floor. I am going to wait here until I hear him leaving.

As I'm waiting, the anticipation is killing me. It feels like I have been sitting here for hours. Out of the blue, I hear the front door open... and then close. Even though the sound of the door opening or closing is getting old, it is all I have to go by. The sound that could lead me to freedom. This could be the sign I have been waiting for. I quickly get up and put my ear to the door. I can't hear anything. I wait a few minutes then walk to the back of the closet where there is a stack of boxes. I take off my sandals. I am so scared. All these different thoughts race through my head and I start to think the worst.

"What if he comes back to soon?"

"What if he catches me?"

"What if that hole is for me?"

Without any further hesitation, I run downstairs to the hidden room and move all the boxes away from the wall where I had seen the light. I push the wall enough to make room for me to squeeze through. I know I can't move the freezer under the window because it's too heavy, so I am going to try to move the tall shelf. I'm hoping I can use it to climb up to get out. I didn't try this the other day, but I wonder if the door to the basement is locked. I quietly walk up the narrow wooden stairs to the door. With each step I take, the boards make a creaking sound. I reach out and grab the knob. I turn the doorknob gently and quietly, while pushing with light force but it doesn't budge. The knob turns, but there must be another lock of some kind because the door will not open.

"Well that was a waste of time," I whisper with frustration. I walk back down the steps and try the shelf. I get my hands placed just right, and start to push the shelf over near the window. The height of the shelf is not making it easy to move. Even though I am moving it slowly, I can't keep it steady. I knock the shelf over causing a bunch of tools and objects to hit the basement floor. They make loud, crashing sounds. The shelf is too heavy to pick up, so I just leave it and run back through the wall into the other room. I swiftly yank the door back, and start carefully putting all of the boxes in their original place as neatly as I can. I race back upstairs hoping he didn't hear any of the noise from the basement. My heart is racing and I can barely breathe. I am not looking forward to him coming in here. This could be the last straw for me. I wait. I wait and wait some more.

"Maybe he didn't hear the noise I caused in the basement," I wonder. "

"Maybe he is gone from the house, or he is outside somewhere and didn't hear anything. That must be it, because he would have been in here a lot sooner if he had."

Not giving up, I use the dumbwaiter. He never locked it back from when I got caught using it last. I bet he did not find the key I had in the pocket of my pants the first day I was here. Which means the door to the dumbwaiter in the attic is still unlocked. I should be able to get out through there. Without further hesitation, I walk to the dumbwaiter, open the door and crawl my way back in. As I inch my way up the shaft, I am sweating from nervousness. I reach the opening and look through the hole in the door. I don't see anyone, so I slowly open the door and crawl out. I close the door to the dumbwaiter and walk over to the small window in the attic. As I lean onto the window to look out, there is no sign of him. But there is a large, deep hole in the ground next to the house.

"That must be what the noise was earlier," I say to myself.

He was using some kind of machine to dig a hole. The hole is narrow and in the shape of a rectangle. I am curious. What does he need that for? Terrified beyond measure, I sprinted over to the attic door. I turn the knob slowly, but it was locked. I yelled softly, "I can't believe the door is locked. How do I get out now?"

I run all over the attic, rummaging through everything I can get through, in order to find something to open the door with. I open the drawer to the vanity table and find a long, thin piece of cardboard that hair pins are attached to. I take the hair pins off to use the cardboard. I walk back over to the door. I slip the cardboard between the frame and the door, deliberately sliding it down towards me. It takes a couple of tries –but it works. I unlocked the door and it now opens. Overjoyed with relief, I open the door slowly and quietly. I can't see down the dark stairwell.

"I'll take my chances," I say to myself, determined to escape. I swiftly walk down the stairs, holding the rails and trying not to make too much noise. Even though, with every few steps, the stairs make a sound as they shift from my weight. I reach the bottom of the second floor, and stand against the door too scared to open it and look around the corner. As I slowly glance around the corner, I can see the coast is clear. I walk across to the flight of stairs on the second floor and look down. It is still clear. Unexpectedly, the front door opens. He's back. I stand back quickly and move around the corner, peeking down at him as he walks in and shuts the front door. He is carrying something, but I can't see what it is. I am so close. I can see the front door, but I just can't get to it fast enough without getting caught. The man goes back towards the front door and walks out, shutting the door behind him. I can make out the blurred image of him through the side window of the front door, and I watch him walk around the porch that is attached to the house. I quickly run down the stairs and go left into the study. As soon as I walk into the study, I realize that I have left my car keys in the closet.

"Oh my goodness, this is not happening to me," I cry out in a low tone. I left them in one of the boxes hidden in with the quilts.

"Think!"

"What should I do next? I need those keys."

I scamper over to the window, looking out careful not to disturb the curtains so he can't see me. I can't see him, so I go over to the other window and look out. I can see him entering the barn. I run as fast as I can out of the study and around the stairwell to the closet door. I unlock it and run in. I head for the stack of boxes, knocking them over to get to the right one. I open it quickly, violently throwing the blankets out. The keys fall from one of the blankets. I quickly snatch them up and walk back over to the closet door. I open the closet door just enough to look out, and it seems to be clear. I walk out, closing the door and locking it back. Then I run silently back into the study to look out through the windows. I need to know where he is. He is coming.

He is on the porch and coming around the corner. There is a large grandfather clock next to the doorway in the study, so I run over to it and stand beside the clock to hide. He walks in through the front door, and I hear his footsteps continue down the hall. It sounds like he is going to the kitchen. I am petrified, but I am so close to escaping. The footsteps start coming back down the hallway towards me... and then they stop. He is at the closet. I hear him unlock the door and open it. I walk away from my hiding spot and look around the corner to the closet. I can hear him throwing things. I know that he is outraged. Without thinking it through, I run to the closet and slam the door and lock it.

"He is locked in the closet," I say out loud. He starts beating on the door. He is a strong man.

"He could beat the door down," I think in a panic I quickly went to the kitchen to grab a chair. In the kitchen there is a horrible stench. The kitchen has dirty dishes piled up on the counters, and bags of trash piled up at the back door. The backdoor can barely be seen because the trash is piled so high. I can't make out what the smell is, but I'm gagging. My eyes are watering. It smells like death, not trash.

Without any more delay, I quickly grab a chair from the kitchen table and run to the closet. There is silence. He is not banging on the closet door any more. As I reach out to grab the door knob to check to see if it is locked, I hear a noise coming from the kitchen. It's the sound of a doorknob being jiggled.

"Oh no!" I yelled. He went through the small room, down the stairs in the closet, and made his way to the basement. I lean the chair enough to get it under the handle and prop it tight for extra pressure in case he tries to come back to this door to get out. I turn around and run back down the hallway, passing the closet and head out the front door. I trip down the front porch steps and land face down on the ground. Slowly moving, I try to get up from the ground. As I stand up, I have a sharp pain coming from my right ankle. I try to take a step. I begin to limp on it. I got some scrapes on my arms too. I didn't let it stop me. I dart towards the barn, limping while my feet are being cut up from running barefoot.

When I reach the barn, I run to the side and push the stack of pallets to line them up under the window. I crawl up on the stack using my elbow and I smash the glass window, breaking it into several pieces. My heart is pumping so fast that I did not realize I cut my arm while breaking the glass. I can hear something. I lean back away from the barn and I can see him coming towards me and yelling.

"How did he get out from the basement?"

I fall in through the window, scraping and cutting my legs up. I quickly unlock my car and get in. I lock the doors, then put the keys in the ignition as fast as I can to start the car. I turn the key but it won't start. It is making noise, but not starting up. It has been sitting here too long without running. I pump the gas a few times and try again. As the car starts, one of the doors of the barn opens in front of me. It's him. He is standing at the door to the barn staring at me. I rev up the engine a few times and continue staring at him. He takes one step toward me. With my right foot on the brake, I shift into drive and gas it. He jumps out of the way as I get close to him, then I ram the other door open smashing out of the barn.

I keep driving - never looking back. My car slid a little as I drove through his pasture towards the road and I wreck through the picket fence. I reach the road and just drive. I don't even look to the left to see if any cars are coming. Overwhelmed with excitement and fear, I start crying and drive straight to the police department, not caring how fast I am going.

I get to the police department and park my car. I put my hands and head on the steering wheel and cry my eyes out.

"I can't believe it worked. I am free," I squealed aloud.

Chapter 6

I jump and scream at the top of my lungs. It is a police officer tapping on my window. Relieved, I open my door and get out. The officer asks, "Can I help you Miss?"

I grab ahold of him, wrapping my arms around him and begin to cry more. Then I say in a stuttering voice, "I need your help."

The police officer moves his arms and puts them around me while he is guiding me toward the police station. We come up to the door and he punches in a code on the key pad. The door makes a buzzing sound, then he grips the handle turning downward. He pulls the door open then says with a calming gentle tone, "Please come in and tell me how I can help you."

Together, we walk down the hall and around the corner to his office. "My Name is Detective Daniel Ward, but you can call me Daniel. Please have a seat."

I walk around the chair, grabbing a tissue from his desk, and sit down. He walks over to the small table in front of the window in his office and pours a glass of water. Then he walks over to me and hands me the glass of water.

"Thank you," I say while taking the glass from his hand. He sits down on the corner of his desk, then he asks with a sincere voice, "What can I do for you?"

As I begin to tell him what happened, I try not to be as hysterical as I was when I first got to the station. "I was kidnapped a few days ago and I was held in a closet before I escaped. The man drugged me also." I said frantically while sobbing a bit.

This strange look came over Detective Ward's face. I can't really describe the look, but he went from a sincere expression to a shocked one without saying a word. Detective Ward asks, "When did this happen?"

I respond, "I escaped and came here."

"Are these the clothes you were in while you were being held captive?"

"Yes, this is what he gave me to change into, along with some other clothes that were left at the house. I was able to get free and came straight here."

"Let me get a female officer to go with you so we can check for anything on you that can be used as viable evidence."

Detective Ward picks up his phone and asks Officer Kelly to come to his office. She enters his office. "Yes sir," she says politely.

"What is your name?" he asks me.

"Lexi Alan," I responded.

"Take Ms. Alan and have her change out of her clothing. Place it all in an evidence bag. Let me know when you're finished."

"Yes sir," the lady repeats.

"Come with me," she says.

"My name is Officer Kelly. I am so sorry for what has happened, and what you went through," She says genuinely.

"Thank you," I reply with a terrified look on my face.

"Here are some clothes to change into, but I need to first ask you a personal question, and I hope that you can answer me. Were you, or do you know if you were sexually assaulted?"

I quickly answered, "No! He never touched me in that way, but he did drug my food."

Officer Kelly said with a sigh of relief, "I am relieved that you did not go through that. Once we are done here and I get your statement, we need to go to the hospital to get some blood work done so we can find out what drug, or drugs, he has given you."

I am standing behind a tall, white curtain and slowly take my clothes off - leaving only my undergarments.

"Here. Put your clothes in this bag, then let me know when you are done. I will be standing right outside the door."

I take the clothes and begin to change. She has given me a grey jumpsuit. It looks like something a prisoner would wear, but I don't care. I would rather wear this than the clothes that monster gave me. I quickly change, put the clothes in the bag, then I yell out to Officer Kelly, "I am finished."

She walks back in the room and has a small box in her hand. "If you will please have a seat, I will collect some evidence on you."

I sit down in the chair and she begins. She takes a small, metal pick looking thing from the box, along with a piece of paper, and scrapes under my nails. She puts the scrapings on the paper. She folds the papers, then places them in small baggies before she seals them up and writes on the outside. Then she starts looking on my arms and around my neck for distinguishing marks. "I notice you have some bruising on your arms along with scratches. Are these a result of being held captive?"

"Yes," I quickly answer. "I also have a cut on my leg from a couple of days ago." I pull my pant leg up so she can take a picture of it, along with a picture of my arm and neck.

"How did you get this cut?"

"I was trying to find a way to escape through a dumbwaiter and I slipped. I cut my arm and leg."

Then the officer asks, "Will you pull the top of your jumpsuit down so I can take a look at your back?"

I unsnap the top of the jumpsuit and pull it down.

"You have some bruising on your back, so I am going to take a few pictures of these also," she says.

I just sit there. I didn't really want to talk. "Ok, I am finished here. You can pull the top of your jumpsuit back on, then come with me. We can get with a few other officers and then get your statement."

The officer and I walk out of the room, into the hall and pass an open area of desks. I can feel everyone staring at me. I just keep looking forward, following Officer Kelly until we stop at

Detective Ward's office. Officer Kelly peeks in and says, "We are heading to the hospital now for blood tests. Will be back soon."

He answers back "Good deal."

Then she turns around to walk back through the station, weaving in and out of desks with me following her. We are heading towards the back of the precinct. As we approach the back door, Officer Kelly waves her hand in front of the camera that is in the upper corner near the ceiling. The door makes a buzzing sound, then she pushes the door open and we walk out to the parking lot where her patrol car is waiting. She opens the back door and I get inside. We pull out of the parking area and continue down the road to the hospital.

"This is just as frightening as being locked in the closet," I say to myself. The metal cage that separates her from me, and the doors not being able to open, makes me feel trapped like before. I have one hand on the seat and the other on the door handle, even though I can't open it from the inside. I can't hold it in any longer. Without thinking, I let out a high pitch scream with my hands on the cage divider then said, "Stop the car and let me out!"

Without hesitation, Officer Kelly slows down and pulls over to a complete stop. I know I've startled her. She gets out of the patrol car and opens my door. I jump out quickly and run around the car to the side of the road. I sit down at the edge of the curb, bending over and putting my head between my legs. Taking slow deep breaths. I feel Officer Kelly's hand on my shoulder as she rubs slowly.

"Are you all right? I didn't think. I should have put you up front with me," she says with a soft and sincere voice.

We sit here for a few more minutes so I can collect myself. I look at Officer Kelly as I get up then say with a pause, "I think I am ready now."

She gets up and we walk to the car. I get in the front passenger seat this time. I feel much better now. We continue driving, heading to the hospital and arriving about twenty five minutes after leaving the precinct. We park close to the front entrance and get out, making our way through the sliding glass doors to the registration desk. We are greeted by a lady. "How may I help you?" the lady asks nice and politely.

Officer Kelly answers back, "I called earlier. We are here to get a blood test administered as soon as possible for evidence in a current case."

"One moment please while I check," the front desk lady says.

She uses the phone to call someone. It takes only a few seconds to find out where we need to go. "Please use the elevator and go to the second floor. Right in front of the elevator where you get off is the nurses' station. They will take care of you from there. I hope all goes well."

We walk to the elevator and get in. Being the germaphobe that I am, I refuse to touch the elevator buttons, so I just stand here. The elevator doors close. Officer Kelly looks at me strangely, then pushes the second floor button. The elevator begins to move. The motion of the elevator is making me feel nauseous. After it stops, the doors open to the elevator and we step out towards the nurse's station. Before we can say anything, a female doctor walks around the corner and greets us. She has her hand out to Officer Kelly, "Hi! My name is Doctor Shay Morgan."

Officer Kelly answers, "Nice to meet you," While shaking the doctor's hand. "You must be here for blood tests. I was informed that you would be coming. I have everything all set up, so just follow me."

We follow the doctor around the corner and down the hall to a room. As we walk into the room, I see that it's a regular hospital room with a gown folded on the bed, and a tray beside the bed with all the medical supplies needed to draw blood.

"Change into the gown that's on the bed and have a seat. I will be right back," The doctor says.

They both step outside of the room so I can change. I change into the gown and put my clothes on the small counter near the bathroom. I move over to the bed and sit down with my legs hanging over the side. A few minutes later, Officer Kelly walks in. She walks over to the window and sits in the chair beside it. She says with a caring voice, "It will all be over soon, then you can move on."

All of this is so surreal. "It's like I am in a dream and I can't control what is going on," I thought to myself.

A nurse walks in and goes to the sink to wash her hands. She sits on the stool beside me and starts putting on the gloves. "Hello, I'm Sarah, and I will be taking your blood samples today. Swing around here with your legs on the bed and lay back. It won't take long."

I move to get all the way on the bed and lay back. She starts putting a tourniquet on my arm, then taps to bring my blood in the veins to the surface. Then the stick. The needle is so sharp, I flinch a little when she puts the needle in. She sets the port up and puts the vial in place to draw my blood. After two full vials of blood, she takes the needle out of my arm and puts a band-aid in its place. Looking at Officer Kelly she say, "You are all set. I will put a rush on these, and will get back with you soon."

Then she turns and looks at me.

"You may change, then you are ready to go… but be sure to take it slow, you might feel a little dizzy."

Without any hesitation, I get up from the bed, grab my clothes and go into the bathroom to change. After changing, the officer and I head down the hall to leave. As we're walking, we reach the corner and run into a man in white scrubs.

"Excuse us, so sorry," Officer Kelly says.

He doesn't respond. He just walks around us with his head down. As he walks by, he has this strange smell about him. It's a distinctive odor I have smelled before. I turn around to look at him and he is about ten feet away, looking at me, then he takes off.

"What a strange and peculiar man," I think.

We continue around the corner to the elevator, and then out of the hospital to the parking lot. We walk to the patrol car and get in. Officer Kelly asks, "What's going on in your mind? You haven't said a word since you changed."

"I can't get the smell out of my head. That smell is all I can think about," I responded. "When that man bumped into us, he had a smell about him that triggered something, but I can't quite put my finger on it."

We start pulling out of the parking lot to drive back to the precinct. Twenty minutes later, we arrive at the precinct office. Detective Ward is outside the back door walking towards us as we park. Before I can get out of my seatbelt, he opens my door then says, "The test results came back. They show two different drugs. One is a sleep aid called Ativan, a type of benzodiazepine. The other drug on the streets, is known as a zombie drug scopolamine. Let's go in my office and I'll explain it more in depth."

We walk into the precinct station after he punches in the code to open the door. We head down the hall to his office and I sit down as he shuts the door. Detective Ward begins to show me information about the drugs found in my system by handing me some papers that were emailed to him that he then printed off. As I read, the pages show what both drugs are used for, and lists what the side effects are. The drug Ativan is a sleep aid used for people with insomnia. "Of all the side effects, the ones that stick out the most are dizziness, drowsiness, and weakness," I said aloud while reading over the test results. "And the side effects of scopolamine... sometimes I could not remember things- things like how long I had been there, even though I was keeping track of it. I was shaky, had blurred vision, and even felt nauseated at times. I need to the use the restroom."

"It's down the hall past the breakroom," Detective Ward says.

I get up from the chair and head down the hall to the bathroom. When I finish, I wash my hands and I use the soap from the dispenser. It hits me-the smell I was thinking of while at the hospital is the soap smell.

The man that almost bumped into us smells like the soap I was using to wash my hands while I was held captive in the house. "This could be something," I realize

I quickly run out of the bathroom, and back to the office. I yell to Detective Ward with excitement, "I know what the smell is that was bugging me earlier. The soap I used while held captive is the same smell from the man we met briefly while at the hospital. There is a hidden room beyond a door of the closet that leads down to a closed off space of the basement. I would wash my hands, and also wash off at the sink because there was no way to shower or bathe. The smell is that of the soap I used."

He just sits at his desk staring at me.

"Don't you get it?" I yell. "It's hospital grade soap. I bet he works at the hospital."

Without further wait, Detective Ward gets up then says, "Let's start by getting your statement then we will go from there. I don't want to jump to conclusions, sending officers here and there... wasting man hours on a hunch."

We walked into the interrogation room where he pulls a chair out and asks me to have a seat. The room has a small table with a chair on two sides of the table, a glass mirror, which is two-sided I am sure, and a video camera in a corner. An officer brings in another chair and sits right beside the camera.

"I guess he will be operating the camera to record my statement," I think to myself.

We begin with Detective Ward saying, "Will you please state your name for the record?"

I respond with a sigh of relief and nervousness.

"My name is Lexi Alan."

"Now tell us what happened. And be as detailed as you can, leaving nothing out."

I begin telling him what happened. "I was driving home from work early because of the storm five days ago. I got stuck in traffic because of the accident that was ahead of me. I just so happened to be in front of this old house. I was staring at it for a bit, when I noticed what looked like a shadow of someone falling on the second floor of the house. I quickly ran to go help. I ran up the steps to the door, but no one answered, so I went around the other side of the house to an open window. I yelled as I climbed in and started searching around. I went upstairs where I thought I saw someone fall, and still found no one. I went back down stairs, and before I knew it, I was pushed into the closet where I stayed while I was captive."

I went on to tell them, "There were many things that happened while I was there, and the conditions and treatments were strange. I found an old journal, medical records, and… oh wait, I even saw a dead body in the basement freezer!"

"Wait! How did you get to the basement if you were locked in the closet?" Detective Ward asks.

"I used the dumbwaiter that goes from the attic down to the basement."

"I see," he says, "please continue."

I continue where I left off, ""While I was in the basement, I went to push the freezer under the window but it was too heavy. I opened the freezer door to see why, and I saw the body of a man wrapped in clear plastic. It looked like he had been there awhile."

"Can you write down the description of the house, and the directions so we can find this house you are talking about?" Detective Ward asks.

He hands me a piece of paper and a pen. I write down the description and directions the best I can, estimating the distance from the city limits of Old Mills Hollow. The detective takes the piece of paper from me and looks it over. He raises his hand up a bit and asked me another question.

"Would you hold just a moment? I will be right back."

The officer operating the camera pauses the recording while the detective is out of the room. So here we are, sitting in this room together with nothing but odd silence between us. Suddenly the door opens to the room we are in and the detective walks back in. He says, "While we are finishing with your statement, I gave the directions to two officers who are going out to check the house and confirm what you're saying."

With frightened hesitation, "Are you going to bring the man in that kidnapped me?"

He answered back, "We can't without a search warrant, and we need some type of evidence of foul play before I can be granted a search warrant. We need solid evidence not just what you claim. It's not that we do not believe you, but there are laws and guidelines my team must go by in order to prosecute the man- or men, that did this to you."

I quickly respond, "I have this letter that was in a journal that I had found while I was locked in the closet. I stashed the journal into a space in the wall inside the closet, but kept the letter."

I took the letter from underneath my bra strap, and hand it to the detective. He opens the letter and begins to read it. Detective Ward quickly darts out of the room after reading the letter. He is gone for what seems like forever. I just want to hurry up with all of this so I can put it behind me. Unexpectedly, the door opens to the room. It is Detective Ward coming back in the interrogation room. He explains why he ran out so fast, "My partner is getting a judge to sign off on a search warrant as we speak. Hopefully we can get to the bottom of this and catch who did this to you."

While I am finishing with my statement, I go on to talk about the details of being drugged, and how I escaped through the shaft of the dumbwaiter. Abruptly, we are interrupted by a different officer at the door.

"Excuse me, sir. There is a call for you, and you really need to take it."

Detective Ward gets up and leaves the room again. The other officer once again stops the recording. I am so exhausted. I put my head down on the table in my arms, and sit there. The detective comes back in and I immediately sit up.

"Good news! The two officers, that were sent out to take a look around at the house where you were kidnapped, are parked at the road several yards down from the house. They are waiting for the search warrant so they can surprise the man at the house and not tip him off by going to ask him questions." Let's go! So we can take a break and have a change of scenery, the detective states."

We leave the interrogation room and walk down the hall to get outside of the Police Station. We step into his car, which is an unmarked Dodge Charger, and drive out of the lot.

"Are we going to where the officers are by the house?" I said with a curious but nervous tone.

"No. Are you hungry?" he answers back.

I sit for a couple of minutes feeling confused. We continue driving until we slow down and park alongside the road at Old Mills Hollow City Park. He puts the car in park and turns off the ignition. Then he looks over at me and says, "Come on."

We get out and begin walking. "I know you have been through a lot these past few days, and justice will be served. Please do not worry so much. You are safe," Detective Ward exclaims with a positive upbeat persona.

I just glare at him with an unsure glance and thinking in my head, "You were not there," but I just keep quiet We walk about a quarter of a mile, heading towards a small food cart. The vendor on the opposite side of the food cart is wearing a red and white striped shirt with a matching pointed hat. He sure knows how to dress the part. He greets us with such a cheery disposition asking, "May I interest you in a soda or perhaps a hotdog with the works?"

Daniel answers the vendor, "Two hotdogs with mustard and relish, along with two sodas and that will be all."

The man hands him one hotdog and a soda, which he then hands to me. Detective Ward gets the rest of the food and we start walking until we come upon a bench and sit down. It is a nice day out, and after noticing some of the scenery in the park, it is really beautiful here. So picturesque. I didn't really think I was that hungry, but I ate the hotdog pretty quick.

"The best food around is what you can find at the small food carts and stands," Detective Ward says with his mouth full of food.

There isn't much conversation going on while we are eating, but the different sounds in the park break the silence around us. The birds are chirping, and you can hear bells ringing from the bicyclists nearby. After some hesitation, I begin asking him questions.

"Have you been here all your life, and what made you become a police officer?"

"Well, I was born here but I was adopted when I was five. We moved about an hour away from here. My adopted father was a police officer, so grew up hearing his stories before he died, and it made me want to become one. Now I can tell my own stories."

He continues, "There was an opening six months ago here, and since it is my birthplace, I thought this would be a good place to settle and get to know my hometown. Maybe find out who all may have known my birth parents."

I ask him several questions without giving him a chance to answer after each, "Is that the short version of your history?"

"Have you looked up information about your birth parents yet?"

"Do you even know if they are still alive?"

I realized I was asking too much. I did not mean to sound so nosey. Daniel turns his body towards me, placing his right arm on the back of the bench, and quickly smiles with a reply to my question.

"I have been trying to settle in my new apartment for six months now. And what that means is, half my belongings are still in boxes. When I came here in acceptance of my promotion, things were a little chaotic since nothing here is the same as back home. It is taking some time to get all my affairs in order. I need to do that before I can focus on my past, but I hope to start looking into it soon."

Daniel starts to ask me something, but a loud screeching noise came over the radio on detective Ward's hip. One of the officers begins to speak, "This is Officer Henson. The judge has approved the warrant. What would you like us to do sir?"

Daniel got up from the bench. "Let's go Lexi. I need to get over to the house."

He quickly grabs my hand, helping me up, then we walk fast. I could barely keep up with him. Detective Ward answers back. "I am on my way. When you get there, stay out of sight until I get there. Wait until you receive further instructions. Let me know when you arrive."

We get back to the car. Detective Ward opens the door for me, and I jump in. He walks around to the driver's side and gets in.

Almost out of breath, he says, "I don't have time to take you back to the station, so you will have to ride with me. You will stay in the car, and stay down when we get there. We don't know what to expect, and I don't want anything to happen to you."

"I have no problem with that," I affirm with no hesitation.

We sped off. We were driving fast, and weaving in and out of traffic. No sirens, just the emergency lights flashing. I am sitting in the front seat- one hand clinching the door, and the other squeezing tight at the edge of my seat cushion as we weave in and out of traffic.

Officer Henson replies on the radio, "I am here. I'm down the road parked behind a patrol car."

"Copy that," Detective Ward answers.

Secrets Under The Stairs

Chapter 7

Moments later we drive up, passing the officer's patrol car, and use the right side passing lane to turn around. After a few cars pass by, we turn around and pull up on the side of the road. We are down from the house, and on the opposite side of where Officer Henson and backup are.

"Remember what I said earlier. Stay put and stay down," Detective Ward repeats back to me as if I am five years old. He then gets out of the car and walks over to where Officer Henson is standing. I can hear sounds of them talking and strategizing, but I can't quite make out the words. All I can tell is, Officer Henson sounds like he is a little cocky.

I slowly peeked my head to look out the window. I can see Detective Ward, Officer Henson, and the other officers conversing. Officer Henson uses his hands a lot when trying to state a fact or express his opinion. He seems like the one who would rather give orders than take them. Detective Ward finishes the conversation, then begins to walk towards the car. I immediately duck back down when he turns to walk towards the car so he doesn't notice me looking at them. He opens the car door on the driver side and leans in.

"We are going to the house. Stay in the car and do not get out. I will turn the radio up a bit so you can hear what is going on."

I slowly peek out of the passenger window, watching as they step away from where we are parked. Detective Ward and three officers head towards the house where the "alleged" kidnapping occurred. Each one with their hands on their weapon ready to draw. It's "alleged" until enough evidence is collected to prove otherwise.

I can't hear anything, but I can see that Detective Ward is talking to the officers by radio as they split up in different directions when they get closer to the house. One officer goes toward the barn, walking slowly among the grass and weeds. He disappears into the tall grass where I can't see him as he approaches the barn. Detective Ward heads up the stairs of the front porch to the door, and the others head around the house to the back. I can't see the other two officers. Detective Ward uses his left hand to knock on the door while the other is still on his weapon. He stands there at the door for what seems like forever. I am so nervous and anxious, I can't stand being in this car just watching them. I watch Detective Ward a bit longer, then suddenly the front door opens. I can see him lean in through the front door with his hand still on his weapon. I can't sit here any longer. I open the passenger door of the car and get out. I turn around and quietly shut the car door. I slowly walk towards the house and to the gate- ducking down so no one sees me. As I look at the front door, it is still open, but Detective Ward is no longer there. He must have gone inside. I quickly open the gate, leaving it open and go up the stairs to the opened front door. I lean in but I don't see anyone. I step inside the house and lean against the wall. My palms are sweaty and my knees are shaking. It's like Deja-vu all over again. Suddenly, I hear a noise in front of me coming from the kitchen. I hurry up the stairs, quietly leaning against the wall and skipping every other step to get up there faster. I tiptoe over to the door that leads up to the attic, and I open it. The door is unlocked so I go through and close the door, locking it behind me.

A hand reaches out of the darkness and covers my mouth, and I hear a whisper. "It's me, Daniel. We are still trying to secure the perimeter and the house. You should not have come in. Just stay behind me."

I didn't answer back. I just got behind him like he told me. "I have checked the attic and all is clear," Detective Ward said softly.

More voices come across the radio.

"Barn all clear," and, "Outside perimeter all clear," say the other two officers.

"Use extreme caution and enter the house from the rear. Check the first level while I finish the second level," Detective Ward tells them. He then turns to look at me. I can sense a little annoyance and aggravation in his voice as he begins to whisper, "Stay close and keep your eyes peeled. There is no telling what this man can, or will do."

I stare directly into his eyes as he speaks to me. We are standing just inches apart. It's as if we have a brief moment - a moment of connection. He opens the door to the attic and sticks his head out- looking left, then right. He is holding his gun with both hands pointing outward, aiming and ready to pull the trigger. He walks out into the hallway and goes to the right to check the next room. I am sticking close to him with my hands on his back, while looking behind us as we are walking. I am so frightened. Detective Ward opens the door, slowly aiming his gun into the room as he turns on the light. We both walk in single file as he looks around to make sure all is clear. He signals me to stay by the door and up against the wall. He walks over to the bed and kneels down to check under it while still aiming his gun. It's clear. Then he gets up and starts walking over to the other areas of the room, ripping at the sheets that cover the furniture. There are no signs of the man here, so Detective Ward walks to the closet. He stands to the side of the closet door and puts his hand on the knob. He turns the knob slowly and throws the door open, aiming his gun. It's a long narrow walk in closet. He walks in. I can't see anything, but I can hear him rummaging through the closet, searching for the man. He comes out looking at me and says, "Clear. Let's go!"

We walk out of the room and walk to the end of the hall where a door is closed. He points for me to stand by the wall on the opposite side of the door while he checks it out. He turns the doorknob and throws open the door. It's a hall closet with shelves, and no room for anyone to hide. He gets on the radio to the other officers and says, "Second floor clear. Heading downstairs."

As we walk towards the stairway, Detective Ward is looking over the banister, ready to shoot. I am walking behind him, matching each step that he takes- shaking fearfully, not knowing what to expect next. We both arrive at the bottom of the stairs. Looking in all directions, and staying alert of our surroundings, he glances quickly to the right, down the hallway. There are French doors that are closed and locked. He then looks around the corner to the left into the study. I stay against the wall at the bottom of the stairs while he inspects the study.

The study is a large open room. The only space for anyone to hide would be under the desk, but no one is here. The other officers meet with us in the study. The first officer stated, "First floor is clear," and the other says, "Barn and grounds are clear."

Detective Ward radios to headquarters, "No sign of the man in question. There is a lot of ground to cover if we are going to get the evidence collected in a timely manner. I need more man power."

Dispatch answers back, "10-4. They are on their way."

In the meantime, we can start collecting evidence. Lexi, put these on. I do not need you contaminating the crime scene from when you were here before."

I grab the gloves and put them on. Then he states, "Show me where you found the body of a man."

"It was in the basement," I answered.

We walk together down the hall and into the kitchen. We go around the island to the door that leads to the basement. He puts his hand on the doorknob, turning the knob slowly and quietly.

"Stay behind me just in case," he says.

He turns on the light switch that is at the top of the stairs, and we begin walking down. We arrive at the bottom of the stairs and he looks around to make sure all is clear.

"It's over here. I found it in the freezer when I tried to push it to the window so I could climb out, but it looks different. It's cleaner than I remember and the shelf I knocked over is back in its place." I anxiously realize.

Detective Ward opens the freezer, and I just stand there in shock.

"Where is it?" I yell.

"The body was right here! It was a body of a white male, maybe early thirties. The body was discolored and looked like it had been here a long time. I know it was here. You believe me don't you?"

Detective Ward says with a puzzled look, "He knew you would tell the police so he moved the body. Let's go back upstairs and show me the room you were held captive in."

We walk back up the stairs, through the kitchen and down the hallway. "This is it. He hit me in the back of the head, and then pushed me in the closet- locking the door behind me," I explained.

Detective Ward puts his hands on the door knob and turns it. It's locked. "Stand back!" he yells.

He raises his right foot up and slams it on the door to the closet, kicking it open instead of checking to see if he can unlock it first. The door slams open and Detective Ward quickly moves inside the closet with his weapon drawn. He positions his flashlight over the gun so he can see better in the dark closet. I take a step into the closet and reach over to the right of the closet. I flip the switch, turning the light on. Ward continues using his flashlight for added light. He checks around the room and it is clear. No sign of the man.

"Walk me through the events of your capture from when you were here, but first let me turn on my tape recorder. Just talk to me and give me as much detail as you can remember," Detective Ward asks.

"First, let me show you the journal I found. I hid it in a space in the wall," I explained.

I walk over to the wall by the table that I made, and pull the piece of wood from the wall. It is still there! Still wearing the gloves Detective Ward had given me earlier, I bend down to grab it from the space. I hand it to him. He takes it from my hand, then calls over the radio.

"I need an officer to the closet underneath the stairs by the front door entrance with evidence bags."

Officer Henson walks in with an evidence collection kit. He puts it on the floor at the entrance of the closet and opens the box. He puts on a pair of gloves then asks, "What would you like me to do first boss?"

Detective Ward answers, "Bag this journal, then wait and listen as Ms. Lexi walks us through the events that took place. I will give you further instructions as needed."

"Yes sir!" Officer Henson replies.

I walk over to the door of the dumbwaiter and open it.

"This is what I used to escape. This leads to each floor of the house. This is how I finally escaped."

Detective Ward walks over and puts his head in, looking in both directions.

"This is a small space," he states with a puzzled look. He signals Officer Henson to process the area of the dumbwaiter for finger prints.

"It was tough to climb in, and I even cut myself, so it's possible you may find traces of my blood in there," I tell them.

Secrets Under The Stairs

I escort Detective Ward over to the boxes that the medical records were stored in. He begins to skim through the boxes and notices a small picture of a boy. He stares at the photograph for a few seconds and then puts it back.

"There is something peculiar about this photograph. Box up these records and put them at the front door," he says to the officer then turns to look at me.

"What else can you tell me?"

I look at him and respond, "I would like to show you something upstairs that I think I figured out while reading the journal."

We walk upstairs to the master bedroom and then into the bathroom. I take him near the bathtub. "Now I don't remember word for word, but in the journal the lady stated that she feels safer in the bathroom. When she takes a bath, she locks the door and uses that time to write in the journal while she has a glass of wine."

I go on to tell him about the two boys.

"She has twin boys, and she believes one is evil. Not evil in a spiritual sense, but a physical and mental sense. David is the one she refers to as evil, and Daniel is the good child- sweet and caring. She gave Daniel up for adoption to keep him safe."

I point at the broken wine bottle, "I think David came in here and hit her over the head with that wine bottle and killed her. What I thought was rust in the tub is in fact blood. I believe that broken bottle is what he hit her with."

Detective Ward replies to my assumptions with curiosity and sarcasm. "Wow! That's some detective work. Maybe you should have my job."

That instant, I get red in the face and turn around to walk out. He immediately grabs my arm to stop me. He turns me back around and we are facing each other.

With his hands on each of my upper arms, he expresses in a sincere tone, "I apologize. You didn't deserve that. Please forget I said that remark."

Here we are again face to face and staring at each other. The moment of silence is broken by a voice over the radio, "C.S.I. is here to collect evidence. Where would you like them to start?"

"Be right there," Detective Ward responds back.

With his hands still on the upper part of my arms, he rubs them in an upward and downward motion then says, "I need to give them some instructions, but I first want to make sure we are fine?"

Secrets Under The Stairs

I'm not sure why he is referring to us like we are a couple. I answered back, "I am fine."

"I want to continue this conversation later- if that is all right with you?" he says with a sad and almost pouty "puppy dog" look.

We turn and I follow him out of the bathroom and through the bedroom. We go through the hall, then down the stairs. We are greeted by Officer Henson as we arrive at the bottom of the stairs on the first floor. As they begin to talk, I walk around them and walk out the front door. I start walking down the steps of the front porch and continue through the gate to the car, taking my gloves off in the process.

Many thoughts race through my mind. With everything that has happened to me these past few days, I don't need some ego driven jerk with a power trip getting under my skin. It's the stress of not knowing where this man is -and when he will be caught, that is making me irritable. I lean up against the car using my back, and cross my arms in front of me. Reliving the events of my kidnapping may help the officers. Standing here for a few minutes, I begin to think back. Suddenly I remember the sounds of a construction vehicle while I was in the closet, which I later discovered was used to dig a hole.

I yell out, "I need to let Detective Ward know."

Without delay, I run back to the house. One of the CSI's stop me.

"I need to see Detective Ward! I remember something that may be of interest to him!"

I rush through my words with excitement. The CSI points to the house. I walk up the steps of the porch and walk to the front door. As I reach out to open the front door, it opens and there stands Detective Ward.

"I was wondering where you went," he says with a voice of curiosity and surprise.

The words fly out of mouth, "I remember something. Follow me."

As we walk, I speak to him about what I remember. I escort him off of the porch and around the side of the house.

"When I escaped from the closet, I looked out the window of the attic and saw that the man had been digging a rather large hole."

Then I pointed right where I had seen it. Detective Ward walks closer to the side of the house and bends down. He is rubbing his hand through the dirt. He gets up and calls over the radio, "I need a few officers with shovels to meet me outside by the house immediately."

He turns to look at me. "The ground has been disturbed recently. We need to dig it up slowly and see if there is anything buried here, or if there are any clues that can lead us to him."

Chapter 8

Two officers arrive with shovels. Detective Ward gives them directions and they start digging. Both officers are digging just inches deep throwing the dirt into separate piles. Other officers are combing through the piles of dirt for evidence when one officer says, "I got something!"

He picks the object up with his glove covered hands and brushes the dirt off. It's a man's wedding band. He puts the ring in an evidence bag and into the collections case. They continue to rummage through the dirt. They now have a hole about six feet deep and five feet wide, still digging when the shovels hit something solid. One of the officers climbs out of the hole. The other officer holds the shovel upside down and scrapes slowly and gently on the surface. As he is scraping the surface, he notices something flip up out of the dirt. He reaches over to inspect it. The object in the dirt is a piece of clothing. He puts the shovel on the ground outside of the hole, and starts digging slowly with his hands to remove the dirt from the area where the clothing is. Many law enforcement officers are standing around the scene, watching suspenseful, waiting to see what is in the hole. The more dirt he removes from the area, the more the hole reveals. Everyone stands in amazement as he reveals the body of a man.

Detective Ward calls for the medical examiner. When they retrieve the body from what is now a burial site, the M.E. can quickly inspect the body to see how long he has been dead, and possibly give the cause of death. Detective Ward walks over to me and asks, "Is this is the body you saw in the freezer that was in the basement?"

Puzzled, I respond, "I am not sure. He was frozen when I saw him in the freezer, but I would remember the shoes he was wearing if I see them again."

As they clear the dirt around the body and get him on a black tarp, I walk over closer to see. Two men lift the body out of the grave and place him on the ground nearby.

"That is it!" I yell.

"That is the body I saw in freezer. I recognize the shoes."

I immediately turn around. I have never seen a dead body before all of this happened to me. Detective Ward walks up to me and asks, "Are you all right? Let's go over here away from this area and sit down."

I sit down on the steps of the front porch shaking. Detective Ward is standing next to me while I am sitting down. The M.E. uses an officers' radio and calls to him stating the cause of death is two gunshot wounds to the back. Ward answers back. "On my way."

Then he looks at me, "Stay right here and I will be back in few minutes."

I look at him and just nod my head. Minutes go by and I am still sitting on the steps thinking of all that has happened. I can't believe he buried that body. I wonder if it is his father. When I saw him in the freezer, there was so much ice on him. He looked so blue and pale. I don't know what possesses me to go back, but I am tired of sitting here so I get up and walk back inside the house and into the study. There are several people in the house going through every inch, and collecting as much evidence as they can. I walk over to the desk and sit down in the chair. I start opening drawers and digging through them. I don't see anything really important that looks like evidence to me. I close all the drawers and get up. Behind the desk is a wall of shelves with books and antique décor. These books have been here a long time. Some of them date back to the early nineteen hundreds, and most of them are history books about ancient times and different countries around the world. I walk around, back and forth, and notice a small section of law books. I wonder if the man found in the grave was a lawyer, or maybe he just needed these for reference. One of the law books seemed different than the others so I grab it, but it doesn't move. It's as if it is nailed down or glued. I put both of my hands on the book and pull it. Suddenly the entire shelf moves and dust blows out of the cracks. Part of the shelf is a hidden door to a secret room. I walk to the opening to look in, but it is too dark. I move the door a little more, but I still can't see.

"I bet no one knows about this yet. I need to go tell Daniel."

I turn around to walk away from the hidden room. Suddenly, I am grabbed from behind. I am being pulled into the room. I am barely hanging on to the doorway of the room. I'm trying not to be pulled in, and I'm screaming loudly, but muffled.

"Help me! Help me!"

Detective Ward and a few officers run into the study. He pulls his gun out and points it towards me.

"Let her go or I will shoot," Detective Ward screams.

It's the man that kidnapped me from before. I can tell without seeing him because of the soap smell, and because of his clothes. He is wearing hospital scrubs. This is the man I saw at the hospital today when I was getting my tests done. I knew there was something about him, but I couldn't put my finger on it. The man puts his arm around my neck. My hands are on his arm trying to hold on so that I don't choke, while at the same time trying to keep my balance. He continues to yell and the other officers also have their guns pointed at the man.

Not knowing what is going to happen next, I had to make a quick choice. I move my feet to the right side of the man and bite down on his arm so hard it draws blood. He jerks his arm enough that I can get loose and get out of the way. Detective Ward moves in fast yelling at the man, "Get face down on the floor now!"

"Do it! It's over!"

I run over to the officers and get behind one of them. The man falls down to his knees and places his hands behind his head.

"Get face down on the floor and put your hands behind your back," Detective Ward yells.

He puts his hands on the floor to balance his weight, lays down and puts them behind his back. Detective Ward rushes over and puts the handcuffs on him, and then helps him get up.

"Get on your feet."

Secrets Under The Stairs

The man gets up and he is escorted towards the door to the study. I move away from the door so that I am not near him. The man unexpectedly pulls away from Detective Ward and tries to lunge at me. I fall to the floor trying not to get hit by him and a shot is fired. He falls to the floor making a big sound. Detective Ward rushes to him to check his pulse. He is still breathing. Detective Ward yells over the radio, "Get a medic!"

He looks at the man and turns him over. "You're not dying on my watch," he says with an angry look on his face.

He stares into his eyes as he waits for the medic, then turns the man over on his side and unlocks the hand cuffs. He takes them off of the man. Then he rolls him on to his back. I am in shock. Why would he take the cuffs off of the man? The officers and I just gaze at him while he is laying there gasping for air. Both of my hands are near my month, close enough to cover my face quickly if I need to. Some quick thoughts come to mind. If he dies, he will win. There will be no way to make him pay for what he did to me and this family. The medic comes in with his medical bag to check him out. He listens to his heart and his breathing, then looks at Detective Ward.

"He can't be saved. The bullet punctured his lung and he is bleeding internally," the medic says to him in a somber tone.

Detective Ward grabs for his hand and holds it while he is laying there. We are in shock while watching him respond to this man the way he is. Detective Ward leans over and whispers something in his ear. We can't hear what he is whispering to him. The man takes a few deep short breaths then closes his eyes as his head falls to the left. The medic checks his pulse then looks at Detective Ward and shakes his head in a sideways motion. He lets go of his hand and walks out of the room.

Chapter 9

I notice that the large picture on the wall of the man pointing his finger is the man that was found in the hole dug up beside the house. I also notice he is pointing to the book shelf that exposes the hidden space beyond the wall. If only I had put that together earlier. I rush to follow him out.

"Are you all right?" I ask Detective Ward as he walks out the front door and down the steps. He sits down on the second to the last step with a lost look on his face, then it all comes out. Detective Ward begins to tell me what he found.

"While you were in the study, I went upstairs to see what Officer Henson had found. It was in the children's room. I walked into the room and started looking around. Some of the things in the room brought back memories of my childhood. I used to have a train set. My brother would always hog the controls so I couldn't man the train. I looked through the toy box and found an old teddy bear with the name "Daniel" sewn on the back of it. I remember sleeping with a bear just like the one I found, and sometimes my brother would take it and hide it from me. He even buried it in the back yard once."

The entire time he is telling me all of this, I am sitting here in shock because I know what he is about to say next.

"After looking through the toy box, my curiosity got the best of me. I had to know. I went downstairs to look through the boxes of medical records that we found in the closet. I checked the dates on them. I remember some of the injuries from when I was little, and it shows the same birthday on the records as mine is today. It can't be coincidence. With all that being said, a blood test will confirm that David is my brother. Ward is the name they gave me when I was adopted. My last name used to be Shaw."

Wow. What Detective Ward, Detective DANIEL Ward just finished telling me puts me in complete shock. I can't imagine my family history being remotely similar to his. I put my hand on the back of his shoulder and give him a quick pat. I don't know what to say to Daniel, especially after being so short with him earlier. We look up and watch as the medical examiner loads David's body into the van. Officer Carroll walks up to us while we are still sitting on the steps.

"After removing the body of the man from the shallow grave over on the side of the house, we dug a little deeper and found the body of a woman."

"If David is my brother, then the other two bodies are my biological mother and father," Daniel replies.

Officer Carroll stood there looking at Daniel like he is confused or crazy.

"What do you mean Sir?" Officer Carroll asks.

Detective Ward replies, "Never mind."

He gets up from the steps and walks around the corner of the house. I get up to follow him. The body of the woman is already in the body bag so he didn't see her. Detective Ward speaks over the radio, "It's getting dark. We need to finish gathering the evidence and clear out. Officer Henson is in charge so see him for questions or direction."

He walks over to Officer Henson. I can't hear their conversation but, I'm assuming he is probably giving him some instructions. Daniel heads back towards me, signaling for me to head his way as if we are meeting halfway. As I approach him, he tells me he needs to head back to the precinct and that we need to leave now. We walk together side by side to the car. He walks around and opens the passenger side door.

"Thank you," I say as I get in.

Secrets Under The Stairs

We drive off. Twenty minutes later we arrive at the precinct without any words having been spoken during the ride here. I continue to keep quiet as I open the door and get out. We walk up the steps to the station and he puts in a code to enter the building. He opens the door and lets me go in first. I walk in and stand over by the wall to follow him since I have no idea where to go next. We walk down the hall through the main area of the precinct to his office. He stands to the side and lets me enter his office first. I walk in and he follows behind me, closing the door. I turn around before I sit down in the chair and he grabs me with one hand on each side of my arms. Before I know it, Daniel kisses me on the lips. I am shocked. It is a soft, gentle kiss. The kiss happens so quick I don't know how to respond, but I could not resist or push him away. The kiss is nice and he smells so good. I close my eyes and kiss him back.

The kiss only last seconds, but it felt like an eternity. He pulls his head back then says, "I understand if you're mad at me, but I have been attracted to you since you first got to the station. I don't know what came over me, but it felt right at the time- me kissing you."

For once I have no words. I stand there while he explains to me his reason for kissing me and I sit down.

"Wow, this is awkward," Daniel says.

Then I respond, "Well, you caught me off guard and I am not sure what just happened… but I liked it."

Daniel walks around his desk and sits down. His cheeks are red and blushing from my response to him.

"All right. We need to get a few more details from your capture to finish your statement," Daniel says, stuttering a few words in the process.

I continue with my statement after our most awkward of moments, which ends up taking about an hour. Daniel turns the tape recorder off then goes on to say, "Once your statement has been transferred to paper, you will look over it and sign it."

"Sounds good, I'm ready to get this past me so I can take the next steps in my life and move on."

"I can get an officer to take you home, or if you wait a few minutes, I can take you home" he adds.

I didn't want to sound eager by saying I can wait so I said, "Either way, it's up to you but I do have my car here. I know you have a lot to finish up."

"Your car was entered in as evidence, so you are without a car until we close the case. If you will follow me to the break room, you can sit in there. I won't be long."

We get up and walk out of his office. We head back down the hall to the break room. Daniel pulls out a chair from the table and I sit down. He puts his hand on my shoulder and says, "I will be back in a few minutes then we can go."

Sitting here in this breakroom is getting boring. All I can think is, "How can I move on from this?" I can't believe all that has happened to me. It has been a nightmare these past few days, but I am so glad it's over. He is dead and can't hurt anyone else. Daniel walks in.

"Are you ready? Sorry, it took a little longer than expected, but we can leave now."

I get up from the table and we walk out. He hollers out to the other officers, "Good work everyone!"

He waves goodbye as I'm following him out of the precinct building to his car. He opens the passenger door and I get inside. He shuts the door then goes around to the driver side of the car and gets in. As we pull out of the parking lot, he glances over to me, "Would you like to get a bite to eat before I take you home?"

I immediately respond, "Food would be great after the day we have had. And a glass of wine to go along with it."

We continue driving for a few minutes until we pull up to the front of a small Italian restaurant. I don't even care that I am still in the jumpsuit that I have been wearing most of the day. We get out of the car at the same time and walk up to the outside gate. There is a small podium with a hostess standing behind it. Daniel tells the hostess, "We want a table for two outside, please."

"Sure, right this way, sir" the hostess says.

We walk over to a small table near the side and sit down. The scenery is nice and intimate. Many trees with strings of soft lights, and flowers of different colors decorate the area outside the restaurant. The maître d approaches our table with a bottle of Pinot and pours us both a glass.

"I will give you a few minutes, and then I will be back to take your order," he explains to us with an Italian accent.

After the maître d walks away, Daniel's cell phone rings. "Detective Ward" he answers.

Daniel is on the phone with a confused look on his face, then his whole demeanor changes. He ends the call and puts his phone back in his pocket.

"Wow! They tested my DNA along with David's DNA, and the results came back that he is, in fact, my twin brother. And the people in the shallow grave are my biological parents. This is not how I wanted to find out about my family history, but now I know. It was also confirmed that he works at the hospital, and there are reports of drugs that were stolen. An investigation has been ongoing for some time to figure out who was stealing the drugs. The two drugs found in your system were the main drugs being stolen, so it is safe to say that David was the one stealing them."

My throat quickly became dry then I responded, "I don't know what to say."

Daniel responds, "Enough about that tonight, let's make a toast."

We pick up our glasses and Daniel makes the toast...

"Here's to new beginnings."

END

About The Author

Karen Nolley grew up in Jacksonville, Texas- a wonderful city of compassionate people, family, and friends. Karen is a warmhearted person with a love for her community and of course, writing. While she has been writing for years, *Secrets Under the Stairs* is her first published novel based on a dream she had. With her creative mind and imagination, she hopes to entertain readers for many years to come. Karen currently lives in beautiful Bullard, TX.

Visit www.IslandEntertainmentMedia.com for more information on getting your book published or to order individual volumes.